Walt Disney World
FLORIDA

Big Albert
Moves In

AUTHORIZED EDITION

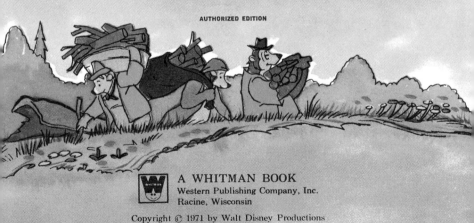

A WHITMAN BOOK
Western Publishing Company, Inc.
Racine, Wisconsin

Big Albert was a shaggy, baggy, wuffly, saggy country bear who lived in the deep woods. He liked honeycomb and wild blackberries and summer rainbows and green hills. But most of all, he liked to sit in the sun and play his guitar and sing.

"Take care, Big Albert!" warned the other bears. "Winter is coming!"

But Big Albert, who was a careless bear, paid no attention. He warbled on in his gruffly way while the green hills turned to gold and the leaves fell . . .

until one day a snowflake plinked down onto Big Albert's nose.

"Oh, my!" he said. "Winter *has* come!"
Oh, but Big Albert scrambled then! He
had to find a nice cozy den, and quickly.
But he was too late. All the nice cozy
dens were taken.

"It is cold here," thought Big Albert.
"And I think it may get colder. Perhaps
I had better go someplace else. Perhaps I
had better go south, like the birds."

Big Albert set out for the South. He walked and he walked, until he was not only cold but tired and hungry as well. Bears get *very* hungry when they do not take care to bring along a bit of honeycomb or a few blackberries.

After a long, long while, Big Albert saw a town.

Now, Big Albert knew that bears really should keep away from towns. But he was a careless bear. He was also tired — and hungry!

"I will sing for my supper," thought Big Albert, and he marched into the town, playing his guitar and singing loudly.

"Look at the funny man in the bear suit!" cried the people, and some of them threw money to Big Albert.

"Now I will eat," chuckled Big Albert. He picked up the money and ran to the market.

"I would like some honeycomb," said Big Albert to the man at the market.

"A bear!" cried the man. "There is a bear in my market!" And he climbed up onto his highest shelf.

"Maybe a blackberry or two?" said Big Albert to the check-out girl.

"*Eeek!* A bear!" screamed the girl, and she fainted.

Big Albert looked out the window and saw a policeman. "Watch out!" shouted the policeman. "There is a wild bear inside the market!"

Big Albert was not really wild. He was only tired and hungry — and very frightened. He ran out of the market, jumped into a truck that was standing beside the curb, and hid.

The truck drove away, and Big Albert curled up in the back and went to sleep. He slept for a long time, and when he woke up, he wasn't cold anymore.

He put his nose out of the truck and peered around.

Big Albert was in a beautiful place
filled with pretty shops and balloons and
popcorn wagons and ice-cream stands.

Big Albert walked down a street, and no one seemed to notice that he was a bear. No one shouted or screamed or called for the police.

Soon he came to a little theater, and he heard wonderful plinking, plonking, twanging, tootling, gurgling music. Big Albert opened the door and went in.

Big Albert could hardly believe his eyes. The theater was full of musical bears. There were bears who played banjos and bears who blew on horns and bears who sang. There was even a bear who played a piano.

"Come in, friend!" called one of the bears when he saw Big Albert and his guitar. "Come join the Country Bears' Jubilee! The music's fine, and the honey-comb's free!"

So Big Albert did just that. And anyone who visits Disney World in Florida today will find him there. And he doesn't even have to worry about the cold winter coming anymore.

Which is just as well. After all, Big Albert always was a careless bear.